"I felt like I was better off not competing. I was going to make a fool of myself in front of the best skaters in the Midwest."

BEN MARTIN
Age: 14
Hometown: Prairie Hills, MN

STONE ARCH BOOKS

presents

TONY HAWK

LIVE 2 SKATE

FEARLESS

written by
BRANDON TERRELL

images by
FERNANDO CANO AND SERGIO MARTINEZ

a
CAPSTONE
production

Published by Stone Arch Books
A Capstone Imprint
1710 Roe Crest Drive, North Mankato, Minnesota 56003
www.capstonepub.com

Printed in Canada.
042014   008086FRF14

Library of Congress Cataloging-in-Publication Data is
available on the Library of Congress website.
Hardcover: 978-1-4342-9147-7
Paperback: 978-1-4342-9144-8
eBook: 978-1-4965-0088-5

Summary: Ben Martin has to overcome his nerves in order to
skate in front of people he doesn't know.

Designer: Bob Lentz
Creative Director: Heather Kindseth

Design Elements: Shutterstock

CHAPTERS

Beep . . . beep . . . beep . . . beep . . .

Ben Martin's hand emerged from the mound of blankets on his bed and blindly searched the nearby nightstand for the chirping cell phone. It knocked over an empty soda can. A stack of *Transworld Skateboarding* magazines. Some bootleg skate DVDs. When it found the bleating phone, it stabbed the screen with one finger until the digital device's daily alarm was silent.

Under the covers, Ben groaned. He stuck his head out, peeled one eye open. The phone display read: 5:31 a.m.

Ben dragged himself out of bed and clicked on the

bedside lamp. Its harsh light cast sharp shadows throughout the messy room. He could hear his father in the kitchen, already up and going, starting the coffeemaker. Ben, who was fourteen, didn't drink coffee, but he definitely needed a blast of caffeine. He reached under his bed, where he'd stashed a pack of energy drinks. He cracked one of the colorful cans open and drank the entire thing in three swallows.

Ben and his parents lived on a farm outside the small Minnesota town of Prairie Hills. Every morning, Ben woke with his dad and completed a few simple chores before heading off to school. Normally, he didn't have a problem waking up at the butt crack of dawn, but last night, Ben had stayed up late watching online vids featuring some of his favorite skaters, guys like Rodney Mullen and Daewon Song.

Ben stumbled into a pair of dirty jeans and a T-shirt. Then he joined his dad in the kitchen.

Gary Martin was filling a metal thermos with coffee. He was tall and broad-shouldered, with the same blond hair as Ben and a thick beard.

"Hey, Dad," Ben said quietly, so as not to wake up his mom.

His dad nodded. "I'll be planting soybeans up by the Nelsons today. Be sure to check the cattle fence before school." Direct. No time for pleasantries.

"Sure thing." Ben's dad walked out the side door of the house as Ben rummaged through the pantry and pocketed a couple of granola bars. Then he pulled on a pair of dirty work boots and went out to do his chores.

The sun was just starting to cast hazy light on the eastern horizon. It wouldn't be up for another hour or so. The morning was damp and chilly and so quiet that Ben got an eerie feeling. Aside from the chirping of a few far-off birds and the rattle of the machine shed door as his dad prepared to start up the tractor, the whole world seemed silent.

Ben trudged through the dew-covered grass along the pasture fence, looking for breaks or weaknesses caused by cattle brushing up against the wood. As usual, there were none. Next, he fed the cattle their morning meal of grains, hay, and barley. The lumbering cows chewed noisily as they ate. Finally, he ducked inside a long wooden chicken coop and collected a basketful of fresh eggs from the two dozen hens that nested there.

As he did his chores, Ben munched on the granola bars and imagined himself as a pro skater, far away from Prairie Hills, grinding rails and carving street courses with the best skaters in the world. It was a halfpipe dream, though. Ben was stuck. Prairie Hills didn't have a skatepark, and his best friends, Carly and Pete, were the only two people he knew who could land a feeble grind.

The sun was up and it was almost time for school by the time Ben's chores were complete. He went back into the house with the basket of eggs. His mom was in the kitchen. She wore jeans and a sweater, and her brown hair was pulled back into a ponytail. She hummed along to a song playing on a radio placed in a windowsill.

"Good morning," she sang as she folded closed the top of a brown paper bag containing Ben's lunch and placed it on the counter.

"Hi, Mom."

"Better hurry up. The bus will be here any minute."

Ben hurriedly rinsed off in the shower. Then he slipped on a white T-shirt, a hooded vest, jeans, and his favorite pair of beat-up Vans.

When he rejoined his mom, she smiled and said, "Have a good day at school, dear."

From the window over the kitchen sink, Ben could see the long, winding gravel road leading toward town. A school bus approached, leaving a plume of dust in its wake.

Ben snatched the brown lunch bag from the counter, along with his backpack and faded charcoal skateboard from the entryway.

"Later, Mom!" he said as he rushed out the door to catch the bus.

After school, Ben coasted down the sidewalk at a brisk pace, the wheels on his deck clacking along the cement. He only had about an hour or so before his father expected him home to help with evening chores. His mom was never late picking him up.

Ben could hear Carly's and Pete's boards making the same noise behind him, like an erratic heartbeat. On either side of them was a line of brick and stone buildings that made up Prairie Hills's Main Street. A hardware store. A barber shop. A handful of antique and clothing stores.

Ben carved right, ollied into the air, and executed a

backside 5-0 grind on a bench in front of the hardware store. The store's owner, an ancient, white-haired man named Frank Weatherby, scowled as they passed.

Carly rode up beside him. She was a smooth, confident skater who could easily keep up with even the fastest skaters. Her purple chrome helmet tried — but failed — to contain her wild, brown hair. "What are you two dopes doing after school tomorrow?" she asked.

"The usual," Ben said. "Homework and helping my dad. Why?"

"My brother is driving over to Skate Haven. He said we could tag along."

"Skate Haven!" Pete rode between them, his mop of hair flopping in the breeze. "I thought that place was a myth. Like the Lost City of Atlanta."

Carly rolled her eyes. "Atlan-*tis*, Pete," she said. "Anyway, Jesse says it's about an hour from here. You guys wanna go?"

Ben really wanted to say yes, but there was no way his dad would let him drive an hour with a bunch of friends just to go skating. "Uh, let me think about it," he said.

"I'm in," Pete said. "No thinking required."

"There usually isn't." Carly brought her board to a scraping stop. Ben and Pete followed suit.

They'd reached their destination: a small storefront with a green awning that read "GALAXY COMIX." On either side of the name was the image of a UFO firing a laser beam. A picture window out front displayed an array of superhero posters and neon signs.

Ben kicked his deck up into his hands and pushed open the glass door.

A bell tinkled as they entered. The comic shop was a cluttered mess of books, games, collectibles in glass cases, and long racks of comics and magazines. Indie rock was being pumped through the store. A skinny college kid named Ike — who practically lived at the store — sat on a stool behind the counter. He was hunched over a graphic novel, reading.

Ike looked up as they entered. "S'up guys."

"Hey," they answered.

Pete beelined for the rack of new comics, while Ben and Carly wandered over to the magazines. Ben picked up the newest issue of *Thrasher*, while Carly snatched a couple of other skateboarding mags, then sat cross-legged on the floor. Ben joined her.

He began to lazily thumb through the mag, checking out photos of pro skaters mid-trick. On one page, Sean Malto soared high above a mini-ramp. On another, Mike McGill executed his patented 540 McTwist on a halfpipe somewhere in South America. Ben thought of all the exotic, amazing places the pros went and all of the fantastic things they were able to see.

Pete sat heavily beside him. In his hands was a stack of comics. "I can't believe it," he said excitedly. "The newest issue of *MagmaMan* is finally out." He held out a comic in which a superhero dressed in tights spewed piping hot lava out of his mouth.

"Hey!" Ike said, "Careful with those, dude. You get your greasy fingerprints all over them and you buy them. *Comprende?*"

"I know, I know," Pete said. Then he buried his nose in the *MagmaMan* comic.

After a minute or two, Carly said, "Yo, guys, check it out."

Ben looked up from the article he was reading as Carly

shoved her magazine into his face. It was folded back, open to a colorful advertisement. "SKATE WITH THE PROS!" the ad read in bold letters.

Ben read the details aloud. "Five lucky winners will be chosen to shred with the pros at the Midwest SkateFest this summer in Minneapolis. So bust out your best moves, send us a video, and you could be in for one *epic* ride!"

"Cool," Pete said under his breath.

"The deadline is August 1," Ben said.

"We should totally enter." Carly was amped.

"Dudes," Pete said. "We should totally take a camera with us to Skate Haven tomorrow and shoot footage of us doing a bunch of moves. It'll be rad."

"Hey! Don't bend the magazines!" Ike shouted at them.

Ben stood, approached Ike, and dropped his cash on the counter. "Keep the change," he muttered, not taking his eyes off the contest ad.

Ben thought about SkateFest the entire ride home. He thought about it during his evening chores, through dinner, and while he tried to do his homework. He couldn't shake it. Here was his chance to show professional skaters and skate teams that he was more than just a farm boy stuck in Nowheresville. He had the skills; he just needed to prove it.

That night before he went to bed, Ben did two things. First, he carefully tore the contest ad out of the magazine and taped it to the wall above his desk. Second, he sent Carly a text: *Count me in 4 Haven 2morrow.*

HONK! HONK!

"Come on, slowpokes! Let's roll!"

Carly's seventeen-year-old brother, Jesse, leaned out of the open driver's window of his pickup. He was parked in the school's lot, just past the line of yellow buses.

With their boards tucked under their arms, Ben, Carly, and Pete wove through the throng of students leaving school for the day.

"Do you have the video camera?" Carly asked Pete.

Pete, winded, answered, "Yeah."

They piled into the pickup, Pete riding shotgun while

Carly and Ben crammed into the slim backseat behind them. Ben had to twist his legs uncomfortably to the side so he would fit. He was the last one in, wedged uncomfortably between the door and Carly.

It's gonna be a long ride, he thought as he buckled up.

Ben had been anxious all day. He'd told his parents he was going to hang with Carly and Pete, but he'd cleverly omitted the part about *where* they'd be hanging. He'd never lied to his parents before, but he really wanted to enter the SkateFest competition, and if he was going to impress the judges, he needed to show off his moves in a place as cool as Haven.

Ben rolled the window down and was hit by the hot afternoon wind. Jesse cranked up the stereo, and they jammed out as the truck wound through gravel back roads and past fields and forests.

After a while, Pete finally said what Ben was thinking: "Dude, are we lost?"

"Not at all," Jesse said. Wind whipped his messy brown hair around. Ben was amazed how much he and Carly looked alike.

Jesse cranked the wheel, and the truck turned sharply onto a gravel road lined on both sides with towering trees. Up ahead, a large gate blocked the way. Above it, a plywood sign had been hung. "HAVEN. ENTER AT OWN RISK," it read in dripping graffiti letters.

Ben's heart clattered around in his chest. The idea of coming out to a hidden skatepark was one thing. But now that they were actually here, the thought of skating in front of all those strangers was terrifying. He took a deep, steadying breath. It didn't help.

Jesse drove the truck past the gate. Just inside, a broken-down car was parked in the weeds. Propped up on cement blocks, it had no windows or tires. Every inch of the car was tagged.

They parked in a small dirt lot filled with beat-up cars and trucks. Loud music drifted through the trees, and a small pathway led into the woods. They walked down the trail, crossing paths with sweaty teenagers heading back to their car. Some were bruised and bloody with road rash.

I'm completely out of my league, Ben thought.

They reached a clearing in the trees. Throngs of

skateboarders milled about. A large bonfire crackled and twisted high into the sky. In the center of the clearing was a huge, homemade halfpipe and a cement bowl. One skater raced up the side of the pipe and spun her way into a perfect backside 360. The crowd around her roared and banged their decks excitedly on the metal coping of the bowl and halfpipe.

"Heads up, newb!" a voice behind Ben shouted. A large skater narrowly missed colliding with him.

Anxiety coursed through Ben's veins. He could feel his cheeks and ears burning red, and he felt like he was going to pass out. It was too much. There was *no way* he could skate in front of all these people. It was too much pressure, all of these strangers . . . *staring* at him. Watching him. Waiting for him to screw up.

Ben tapped Carly on the shoulder. "I'm gonna head back to the truck!" he shouted into her ear.

"Why?"

"I feel like I'm going to blow chunks."

Carly wrinkled her nose. "Ugh. Go, before you puke on me." Ben lowered his head and wove his way back through the trees to the parking lot.

For more than an hour, Ben lay in the bed of the truck, staring at the sky and listening to the park's heavy metal music drifting through the trees. Finally Carly, Jesse, and Pete emerged from the woods. Carly was showing off her arm, which now sported a large, purple bruise. She was tough and wore her injuries like badges of honor. Pete was reviewing footage on the small screen of the video camera.

When Pete saw Ben, he called out, "Dude, you totally missed out!"

"Yeah, you could have shown most of those posers up," Carly added.

Ben shrugged. "Next time." Though he knew already that there would never be a *next time*.

* * *

The sun was lowering in the sky as Jesse's truck made its way back toward Prairie Hills. Ben's frayed nerves were finally starting to calm down. He just wanted to get home before his parents found out where he'd been. He closed his eyes and laid his head back on the seat.

Bang!

The noise ripped through the truck's cab like a gunshot.

Ben jolted forward as the truck swerved to one side. Jesse wrenched the wheel back and forth, fighting for control of the pickup. "Whoa!" he shouted, slamming on the brakes.

"What happened!" Pete cried out, terrified. He gripped the dashboard with both meaty hands.

"Flat tire," Jesse said through gritted teeth. He brought the truck to a stuttering, safe stop on the side of the road, and they all climbed out.

They were in the middle of nowhere, with fields on every side. There were no cars in sight. As they expected, the truck's front right tire was completely blown.

"So . . . um, what do we do?" Pete asked.

"Duh," Carly said, "We change the tire."

"One problem with that," Jesse said, looking guilty. "I don't have a spare."

Another wave of anxiety crashed against Ben. His hands began to shake, and he shoved them into his pockets before his friends noticed. "You mean we're trapped out here?" he asked.

"Nope." Jesse waved his cell phone at them. "I've got a signal. We can call for help."

"Call who?" Carly asked. "Mom and Dad are out at dinner, and they don't have a cell phone."

"And my mom's at work," Pete added.

Ben came to a sudden, horrifying conclusion. The thought of it was so terrible, it made his mouth dry up, and he could barely speak. "We'll have to call . . . my dad," he croaked.

Busted.

GROUNDED

It was dark by the time Ben's dad's headlights appeared in the distance. When Ben had called, the only thing his dad had asked was, "Where are you? What's the nearest mile marker?" He hadn't sounded angry, but Ben could tell he was in a ton of trouble.

Ben's dad changed the flat tire under the piercing glare of his headlights, taking no time at all. As he rolled the flat into Jesse's truck, he said, "Ben, you're coming with me."

The ride home was long and silent. Ben clutched his board and spun its wheels nervously. He opened his mouth to apologize a couple of times, but the words never found a way out.

They parked in the garage. As Ben climbed out of the truck, his father turned to him, held out his hand, and said, "I'll take that." It took a second for Ben to realize what his father meant. Then he passed the skateboard over. "You're grounded for a month."

"But that's the rest of the school year," Ben argued.

"No skateboarding. You hear me?"

Ben nodded.

"Good. Now go get cleaned up and ready for bed."

"Yes, sir," Ben said quietly.

He sulked to his room and sat heavily on his bed. In the lamplight, Ben could see the SkateFest promo he'd taped to the wall. He tore it loose, crumpled the paper into a ball, and threw it angrily at the wastepaper basket. Then he flicked the light off and buried his head under his pillow.

* * *

Chores. School. Chores. Homework. Sleep. Repeat.

That was Ben's life. Sure, it was only for a month, but even a day without his board felt like an eternity. His dad had locked the battered deck in his office cabinet. So while his friends skated through town after school and hit Galaxy

Comix, Ben was out mowing hay or feeding cows. Pete and Carly had barely gotten a slap on the wrist for their trip out to Haven. But they also hadn't lied to their parents about where they were going.

Pete cut together the footage from their trip to Haven, and one day during lunch, he propped his old laptop on the cafeteria table and played the videos he'd submitted for Carly and himself. It looked so cool. Ben was insanely jealous of his friends.

On the first day of summer vacation, Ben came inside from his morning chores to find his skateboard resting on the kitchen table. At first, he thought he was seeing things, like how a thirsty person trudging through the desert imagines a pool of cold water and palm trees. But then his father spoke from behind him. "Don't make me regret this choice," he said.

"I won't, sir."

"Your chores come first. Hear me?"

"Loud and clear." Ben snatched the board off the table. He ran his hands along the grip tape and rapped his knuckles on the faded wood. It felt good to be holding it again.

Two hours later, Ben was carving down the streets of

Prairie Hills with Pete and Carly for the first time in over a month. He felt free, liberated at last. They hit the comic shop, where Pete blew his entire allowance on a stack of used *Astro Dad* graphic novels. Then they rode to the middle school at the edge of town.

There were a few cars in the parking lot, but otherwise the school was deserted for the summer.

"First day out of the place, and we're already back," Carly said, kickflipping off a curb and into the parking lot.

"That's because it's the best place in town to skate," Ben said, nodding in the direction of the school's front steps. Three long, metal handrails lined the stairwell. Along one side of the building, there was a low retaining wall, perfect for practicing boardslides and grinds.

They spent over an hour riding around the school, lazily pulling off tricks. It wasn't even about landing a move; it was the act of doing it. There was a freedom to skateboarding, when your mind cleared and nothing mattered but the board beneath your feet. After a number of unsuccessful attempts, Ben finally ollied into a 90-degree turn with his back truck going over the rail, landing in a backside lipslide.

They broke from riding to lie in the grass of the school's practice football field and bask in the sun's warmth. It was hot, and Ben was drenched in sweat.

After a long silence, Pete was the first to speak. "You know, B, there's still enough time to enter the SkateFest competition."

"I know," Ben said, "But what do we shoot a video of? Me grinding off a bike rack? Heelflipping from a curb? Not very memorable."

"Yeah, it's not quite the same as hitting the halfpipe at Haven," Carly agreed.

"Exactly. And there's no way my dad will let me go back out to that place."

"Sorry, dude," Pete said. "I wish there was a way we could bring Skate Haven to us."

Carly sat up so quickly, Ben thought she'd been stung by a bee. "That's it," she said. Her eyes were wide, and a mischievous smile curled the corner of her lip. "Pete, you're a genius."

"I am?" Pete looked dumbstruck.

"Uh-oh, Carly's got heatstroke," Ben said.

She cuffed him in the chest playfully, knocking the wind from his lungs. "I know *exactly* what we need to do," she said. Then she leapt to her feet, slid her deck under her feet, and pushed off. "Come on!" she shouted as she rocketed down the street.

Ben and Pete hurried after her.

BUILDING DREAMS

"It's . . . an empty barn." Pete's face scrunched up in confusion.

They were at Carly's family farm, which was about a half mile west of the Martin farm, standing in what was, in fact, the hollow shell of an abandoned barn. Carly's dad had recently built a larger barn on the far side of the property that was more accessible for the tractors and tools he stored inside it.

The relic they currently stood in had been stripped of whatever usable oak and metal it had, leaving nothing behind but brick walls, a cement floor, and a high roof framed with scorched support beams.

Carly had her arms outstretched and a smile on her face. "That's right. An empty barn. It's also where we're going to build our own Haven."

Ben laughed. "We're going to build our own skatepark?"

"Why not? There's all kinds of blueprints online for halfpipes, grind rails, fun boxes, you name it."

Pete was skeptical. "And . . . we're going to build this magical halfpipe with what?"

Carly led them to the back of the barn, where a tall stack of two-by-four boards was piled. "Dad salvaged what he could from the barn. It's still usable."

Ben could suddenly see it. There was time; they could build the halfpipe, record him doing tricks on it, and send it in to the competition. A homemade halfpipe in an abandoned barn? That was bound to grab the judge's attention.

"Let's do it," he said, high-fiving Carly.

Pete asked, "When do we start?"

The following morning, Ben rushed through his chores. Not too quickly, though. He didn't want to miss something upset his dad by shirking his responsibilities. When he was done, he wolfed down breakfast, stashed his board in his backpack — along with a hammer and a box of nails from his dad's machine shed — and pedaled off down the gravel road on his bike.

As he skidded into Carly's driveway, a vehicle crunched along the gravel at his back. Ben turned to see Jesse waving from his open window. As the truck pulled up alongside the hollow barn, he noticed its bed was filled with four-by-eight-foot sheets of plywood.

"You didn't think I'd let you guys build this all by yourselves, did ya?" Jesse asked.

Inside, Carly was showing Pete two pieces of white paper with designs on them. When she saw Ben and Jesse, she waved the paper over her head. "Let's make ourselves a halfpipe, boys!" Her words echoed in the empty wooden building.

For the next week, Ben spent every spare moment he had over at Carly's working on the halfpipe. They used the salvaged two-by-four boards to make a curved, skeletal frame. Then, they built a set of platforms and supporters for each side of the pipe. Jesse helped them. Occasionally, a couple of his friends would join in building the halfpipe, or use other

scrap materials to make as many fun boxes and grind rails as they could.

When the framework was finished, they hammered on two layers of the plywood, carefully bending it so the wood wouldn't splinter. Then they finished the pipe by adding metal poles as coping on both sides.

It felt good, sawing and hammering, sweating and bleeding. They were building the gateway to their dreams.

When the halfpipe was complete, it was over eight feet tall on both sides, and it took up a large chunk of the barn floor. The rest of the hollowed-out space was filled with the makeshift fun boxes and grind rails.

They stood together near the door, marveling in their work.

"Well," Pete said, clapping his smudged hands together. "Who wants to try it first?"

Ben stepped up, snatched his board, and climbed a ladder they'd placed behind one side of the vert ramp. The plywood creaked under his feet, but he never felt like it was going to collapse.

"Smile for the camera!" Ben looked down and saw Pete was now wielding his video camera. The red record button glowed brightly.

Ben took a deep breath and stood at the edge of the coping. "You can do it, B!" Carly shouted.

Jesse followed with a loud, "Rock it, dude!"

Ben stepped on his deck and dropped in. The plywood was a bit rough, but the ramp rode well. Ben made a couple of passes, gaining speed. Then, when he was going fast enough, he shot up from the coping and stretched his front leg and board in front of him in an indy grab. The landing was a bit shaky, and he could feel the ramp move back and forth. He adjusted for this on the next pass, then whipped around in a frontside 360.

Watching from the sidelines, his friends hooted and hollered. Carly banged her deck on the cement floor, like they'd seen the skaters at Haven do when they liked a particular move.

Ben followed up his 360 with a couple more passes. He could sense Pete and the camera getting up close and personal, so he carved over to the side of the ramp, until his wheels blazed right past the videographer. Then he soared off the transition and executed a rocket air by holding onto the nose of his board with both hands and placing both feet on the tail.

When he came to a screeching halt atop the coping once more, out of breath and sweating, Ben felt amazing. He took

REC •

an exaggerated bow, kissed his deck, and threw it toward the camera. Pete laughed, easily dodging the board.

They spent the rest of the day in the barn, pulling off tricks on the halfpipe and fun boxes. Pete shot a large amount of footage, getting shots of Ben pulling off a hurricane grind on the rail and a 5-0 grind from a fun box. In a moment of inspiration, Ben even dragged in the trunk of a weathered pine tree, propped it on two rails, and slid the base of his deck along its rough bark in a boardslide.

When all four of them were sweaty, worn out, and hungry, Jesse told them he'd drive them into town to nosh at their favorite restaurant, the Hill Diner. As they closed the blackened, wooden door of the barn with a resounding slam, Pete shouted, "That's a wrap!"

With the footage they shot that afternoon, Pete cut together a wicked video, and just like that, Ben was officially a SkateFest contestant.

Weeks passed while they waited to hear about the competition. Ben continued to wake up early every morning to do his chores. Then he'd meet up with Pete and Carly, and they would either skate on their vert ramp, hit the comic shop, eat at Hill Diner, or bike to a secret beach on Prairie Lake and cool off in the water. Sometimes, the three of them would be having so much fun basking in the summer sun, they'd forget all about the competition. Often, though, they

talked about SkateFest, and about what they would do if any of them became pro skaters.

Through it all, there was a small voice in Ben's head that kept nagging him. *You couldn't even handle the crowd at Skate Haven*, it whispered, *what makes you think you'd be able to even pop an ollie in front of a crowd as huge as SkateFest's?* He tried not to agree with the voice, but the idea was lodged somewhere in his brain. And it wasn't shaking free.

One morning, as Ben was hunched over in the chicken coop plucking brown eggs from the line of nests, his cell phone began to ring. The sound surprised him. He straightened up, banging his head on the coop's wooden ceiling. He cried out in pain, startling the hens. Then he dug out his phone and saw Pete's ugly mug on the screen.

"S'up?"

There was a brief millisecond of a pause, and Ben knew exactly why Pete was calling. "I heard about the contest," Pete said. His voice was a near whisper. Ben's heart began to race.

"And?"

"You're in."

Ben nearly dropped the phone. Goosebumps rose on his neck and arms. He could practically feel the blood coursing through his veins in equal parts excitement and anxiety. "Shut up," he said.

"No lie, dude. I'll forward you the e-mail. You're one of the top five. Congrats."

Ben tried to contain his excitement, but he couldn't. He let out a loud, whooping holler. Once more, the agitated hens clucked and frantically waved their wings.

Pete laughed. "Dude, meet us at Hill Diner in an hour to celebrate. Milkshakes are on you."

He was alone in the barn. It was dark. The only light came from the moon. It cast a blue glow on the wooden vert ramp. From above, a spotlight suddenly enveloped him and a voice said, "Ladies and gentlemen, Ben Martin!"

"What are you waiting for?" Pete asked from beside him, shoving a board at Ben's chest. How he got there, Ben didn't know. But he was there now. Carly, too. And Jesse. And his parents. They all pointed to the vert ramp, which was also bathed in light.

Ben climbed the rickety ladder on the back of the ramp's platform. When he reached the top, he realized he was much higher in the sky than he should be. The barn had disappeared, and the ramp was out in the middle of a forest clearing, like it was at Haven. It was also surrounded by people. First a hundred. Then a thousand. A sea of people. Then an ocean.

They were all chanting his name, waiting for him to skate. He couldn't do it. His legs felt like cement. Ben looked down and was not surprised to see they actually were cement. His lower half was a statue.

He was rooted in place.

The crowd turned on him. They began to shout, "Boo!" They threw things at him, pelting him on the arms and legs. The noise was loud, deafening. Ben covered his ears and eyes. He opened his mouth —

— and gasped, bolting upright in bed. He was covered in sweat, and for a moment, he couldn't catch his breath. The dream was so intense, so *real*.

He didn't sleep a wink the entire rest of the night.

* * *

"Dude, it was just a dream," Jesse said. He was seated with his legs dangling off the side of the vert ramp.

"What if it's, like, a premonition?" Ben stood on the

opposite coping, rolling his deck back and forth under one foot. "I don't think I can do this."

"Sure you can. We drive up, you step up on that ramp, you skate, the crowd cheers, and we drive home. Cakewalk."

"Yeah, about that. Um, my parents are driving us up." When Ben had told his parents the good news, he'd been met by equal parts excitement (his mother) and grumbling (his father, naturally). They hadn't denied Ben the opportunity, but his dad refused to let the kids drive themselves up to the Cities, not after their fateful trip to Haven. "Not a snowball's chance in you-know-where," were his exact words.

"Oh. That's cool," Jesse said, shrugging. "We'll roll up in the minivan, then. They won't know what hit them." He took the last swig from a can of soda, crushed the can, and chucked it across the barn into a barrel filled with garbage.

"You make it sound so easy," Ben said.

"This is a once-in-a-lifetime chance, bro," Jesse said. "It'll be killer."

"If you say so."

Ben dropped into the pipe, gaining speed. Then he spun himself in a melon air by holding onto the deck's backside.

It was loose, though, and he almost had to bail. The board wobbled under his feet, so the next time up the transition, he grabbed the coping with one hand, his board with the other, and performed a simple invert to steady himself.

It didn't work.

Ben's arm buckled, and he had to let go of his deck. It clattered down the pipe as he struck the plywood hard on his side. The impact knocked the wind from his lungs.

"Yo, B! You okay?" Pete asked. He and Carly were just walking into the barn, carrying grease-stained takeout bags from Hill Diner.

Ben stood and stretched. His left arm was banged up with road rash, and it throbbed painfully. Ben shook it back and forth, wincing.

"I told you," he said, kicking his deck. "I'm better off not competing. I'm just going to make a fool out of myself in front of the best skaters in the Midwest."

They skated for the next few hours, but Ben could never get into a rhythm. He fell more often than he landed, and by the time he kicked up his board for good that day, he had added a few new bruises to his collection.

The following days weren't much better. Ben's confidence was at an all-time low. No matter how much time he spent trying to land a trick — even easy tricks, things he could do in his sleep, like frontside 50-50 grinds or ollie 360s — were a problem. His friends did their best to cheer him on, but he could see in their faces that they were losing hope, too.

The night before the competition, after he'd finished his chores and his parents had gone to bed, Ben snuck out of the house and jogged down the road to Carly's place. There were no lights on; she and her family were fast asleep. Ben slipped into the barn and quietly closed the door.

Jesse had set up a floodlight in one of the rafters. Ben clicked it on, washing the vert ramp with a white glow that made it look eerily like it had in his nightmare.

Ben climbed the ladder and stood on the platform. He toed his deck, then climbed aboard and dropped into the ramp. After a couple of passes, he lifted himself into a backside 180, bracing himself for a hard landing.

His wheels hit the ramp perfectly.

He skated for a while, cautiously at first, then gaining

confidence enough to try complicated moves like grabbing the heelside of his board and bending his knees to the deck nose in a stalefish. He nailed them all.

It's because there's no pressure, he thought. *There isn't anyone watching.*

Only that wasn't exactly true.

When Ben saw the figure silhouetted in the barn door, he nearly leapt out of his skin. Then he noticed broad shoulders and a bald head, and he realized it was his dad.

Busted again. "Uh, hey, Dad," he said.

Gary Martin stepped inside the barn. He placed his hands on his hips. "Little late to be out, isn't it?"

Ben climbed down the ladder and tucked his board under one arm. "I . . . I was just . . . practicing for tomorrow."

"What you need is rest. Come on."

"Yes, sir."

Ben turned the floodlight off and followed his father out of the barn. They walked back onto the empty gravel road. The blue light cast by the moon lit their way home. In the weeds along the ditch, bugs hummed and buzzed. Ben saw a few fireflies in the air. They glowed bright, then faded.

They walked in silence. Ben waited for his father to chastise him, to ground him, to forbid him from competing at SkateFest.

Instead, his father asked, "So Ben, why do you like skateboarding so much?"

Ben was thrown for a loop. His father had never asked him anything so personal before. He had to think about the question for a moment. "I don't know," he finally said. "With so many things, you're just a part of the whole. But with skating, it's just you and the board, and every tiny movement means something. Where you place your feet and your hands. How the deck rotates. How you land. It's grace and motion, and when you land a maneuver, you feel free and fearless all at the same time."

His dad placed a hand on Ben's shoulder. "Remember that tomorrow," he said.

"I will."

"You'll do great, Ben."

"Thanks, Dad."

They walked the remainder of the way home in silence.

After a restless night, Ben ate a light breakfast. He was afraid the eggs and bacon his mom made would make a return appearance shortly after he ate them. Then the Martins piled into their minivan and began the long drive to the Twin Cities. They picked up Carly, Jesse, and Pete on their way out of town. Ben was so nervous, he spent most of the trip with his headphones on, listening to music.

The SkateFest people had said to arrive an hour before the contest winners were set to skate. When they reached the Mall of America, they knew why.

On one side of the mall, there was an expansive,

fenced-in parking lot the size of three football fields. It was packed with skaters. When he saw it, Ben's fright ran cold through every vein in his body.

Why did I think I could do this? I must be out of my mind.

His dad found a spot to park, far from the crowd and with a fair amount of grumbling. Pete clutched Ben on both shoulders and said, "You ready, dude? This is going to be *epic!*" He practically had to shove Ben to get him out of the car.

When they reached the entrance to SkateFest, Ben saw how "epic" it really was. On one side of the lot, a stage had been set up. Massive black speakers flanked it, and a rock band was performing at ear-piercing levels. In another, representatives from skate companies and teams had booths set up. They were selling boards, shirts, and gear. Ben recognized many of the teams. He even saw a few pro skaters, like Minnesota native Alex Majerus. Food trucks lined the parking lot, and many skaters were already noshing on tacos and burgers. As they passed through the main gate and entered SkateFest, a large airplane roared past on its descent to the nearby airport.

In the center of the whole thing was the coolest, largest vert ramp Ben had ever seen.

He turned on his heel, about to dash back to the car. But his friends were there to block him.

"Come on," Carly said. "Registration's right over there."

She pointed to a white tent with a table under it.

They wove through the massive crowd. If Ben hadn't been quaking in his shoes, he would have laughed at how comical it was seeing his parents walking through the horde of skaters.

With a nudge from Carly, Ben stepped under the tent. A woman holding a clipboard stood behind the table. She had short, pink hair, a variety of piercings, and an abundance of energy.

"How can I help you?" she asked.

"Um, I'm uh, Ben . . . Ben Martin."

The woman grinned. "Ah! You're the dude with the homemade halfpipe. Gnarly moves, kid. Here." She slung a lanyard with an ID badge over his head. "Line-up's in thirty minutes. You ready to rock the ramp?"

No. "Yep."

"Cool. There are a couple of the other contest winners. Topher's from Chicago, and Lana's up from St. Louis." She tossed a thumb over her shoulder, and Ben saw two skaters wearing identical badges standing on the far side of the tent. One was a lanky teenage boy about Ben's age. The other was a short, muscular girl in her twenties.

Ben hung around the tent, too nervous to speak to any of the other winners. Two other skaters joined them: a Hmong girl from Saint Paul named Moua and an olive-skinned boy from Detroit named Danny who looked like a brisk wind would carry him away. When all five of the contest winners were present, the pink-haired girl spoke into a walkie-talkie. Then she waved them all together.

"Listen up! Follow me out to the ramp. Here we go, everyone!"

As the skaters ahead of him began to file out of the tent, Ben remained motionless. His frazzled nerves were getting the best of him. Then the skater behind him, Danny, poked him on the shoulder. "Dude, get the lead out," he said. "You're holding us up."

Ben took a deep breath and stepped out of the tent.

The crowd cheered as the five contest winners stepped out onto a platform set up beside the vert ramp. A large screen behind them projected their every move.

An announcer, a guy in his thirties with tattoo sleeves and a gray shirt bearing the red SOTA logo, stepped up. He spoke into a microphone.

"Welcome, everyone, to the fifth annual Midwest SkateFest! I have behind me the winners of the amateur vid contest. We had a ton of entries this year, but these five really know how to shred."

One by one, the contest winners were announced. When Ben's name was called, he stepped forward and waved. The screen projected images taken from his vid, shots of him in the barn on the ramp. The crowd really dug it, and when Ben looked down at Pete, there was a proud smile plastered on his friend's face.

The first skater to show off his moves on the pipe was Topher. The slender teen had zero problems showing off in front of the crowd. His movements were fluid, and he looked at home on the halfpipe.

Moua went second. Ben thought she seemed a bit timid, but when the young girl dropped into the pipe, all of her shyness disappeared. She was an aggressive skater, ending each of her tricks with an exclamation point. She would be a hard act to follow.

Which is why Ben's stomach sunk when he heard the announcer say, "Ladies and gentlemen, our next contest winner comes straight from Prairie Hills, Minnesota. Give it up for Ben Martin!"

Ben slowly climbed to the ramp's platform. His knees felt like Jell-O. He stood atop the coping, frozen with anxiety, for what felt like an eternity.

I can't do this.

Ben looked down, and for the briefest moment, he locked eyes with his dad. He thought back to the conversation he'd had with his father the night before. *"With skating, it's just you and the board up there,"* Ben had said. *"And when you land a move, you feel free and fearless all at the same time."*

Fearless, he told himself. *Be fearless.*

Ben focused on the ramp and tried his hardest to ignore the crowd of people watching him. Then he stepped on his deck and plummeted down the transition.

Ben moved faster than he'd ever skated before. He hit the opposite transition quickly, and he rocketed into the air. He had plenty of time to execute his first move: a frontside flip. He almost over-rotated, and when he wobbled on the landing, he could hear the crowd gasp. He shut them out, focused on correcting his stance, and continued. He raced

up the other side, hitting the coping and pushing down on his nose, a move called a rock 'n' roll. The crowd cheered when he kickturned back down onto the ramp.

For his last run, Ben wanted to wow the judges. His confidence had returned, and as he lifted into the air, he spun in a 360 judo air, grabbing the board with his backside hand and kicking his front foot forward. When he stuck the landing, the crowd erupted. Their roars lasted until after he'd dismounted on the top of the platform. There, he raised one arm into the air and waved. He spied his parents and friends right up front, small faces in a massive crowd, and smiled down at them.

He'd done it.

* * *

The remaining two skaters pulled out all the stops. Lana used her stocky frame to her advantage. Her maneuvers were some of the tightest and fastest Ben had ever seen. And the slender Danny floated above the ramp, making it seem as though he'd never come back down.

Finally, the announcer stepped back onto the platform beside the ramp. Ben and the other competitors lined up behind him. "Oh, man! What a gnarly display of moves. Let's hear it for all our amateur skaters!"

Ben and the others waved once more to the crowd. He couldn't believe it. He'd faced his fear head-on, and conquered it. It hadn't mattered that he was scared, because bravery trumped fear any day.

He joined his family and friends in the crowd.

"Nice moves, B!" Pete said, punching him on the shoulder.

"Wicked," Carly added.

"Thanks, guys," Ben said. He looked over at his mom and dad.

His mom smiled from ear to ear. "We're proud of you," his dad said.

Ben's skating attracted many admirers. As he and his friends relived every second of his run on the halfpipe, three different skate reps stopped and handed him their business cards.

One, a guy whose team was based out of Chicago, smiled and said, "We'll be keeping an eye out for you, farm boy."

Ben was too amazed to respond.

The crew from Prairie Hills stuck around SkateFest for

most of the afternoon. They watched the pros skate on the halfpipe and ate lunch from a food truck serving gourmet burgers and hot dogs. Heck, at one point, Ben even saw his dad . . . *smiling.*

By the time the Martins had dropped off Ben's friends and pulled the minivan back into their gravel driveway, it was already dark. As Ben climbed out, he took a moment to look up at the wide, starry sky. It was quiet but for the buzzing of insects, and now more than ever, Ben loved the calmness of it. He looked up and took in the galaxy of stars winking back at him.

Sure, his dreams of becoming a pro skater were still a long way from coming true. Today had been an amazing step forward, though.

His future was as expansive as the horizon in front of him.

Ben skates with much more confidence since his appearance at SkateFest. He's even managed to nail a few sessions at Skate Haven — with his dad's permission, of course.

L2S Fearless

L2S Martin Hawk Face

L2S Confidence

SKATE CLINIC:
50-50 GRIND

1. Approach the ledge in an ollie stance, going a comfortable speed. The faster you go, the farther you will grind.

2. Ollie up onto the ledge and lock your trucks down.

3. While you grind across, stand up straight, but keep your knees bent. Use your arms to balance.

4. At the end of the ledge, drop off and ride away.

SKATE CLINIC:
TERMS

5-0 grind
a move where a skater pops onto an obstacle, then grinds his or her back truck along it and suspends the front truck above the edge

feeble grind
a move where the skater grinds a rail with the back truck, while the front truck hangs over the rail's far side

frontside flip
a move where, while in the air, the skater grabs the edge of the skateboard between the trucks with the front hand. While grabbing the board, the skater then extends his or her body so the chest faces away from the board, which is pulled behind the skater. The free arm is flung out to the side.

hurricane grind
a grind that starts with an ollie 180, then the back truck (which is now in the front) is placed on the obstacle with the nose pointing back, down, and toward the obstacle

indy grab
a grab where the rider places his or her back hand on the toeside of the board

kickflip
a move where the rider pops the board into the air and flicks it with the front foot to make it flip all the way around in the air before landing on the board again

McTwist
a move where the skater approaches the ramp wall riding forward, goes airborne, rotates 540 degrees in a backside direction while also doing a front flip, finishing in a forward position

ollie
a move where the skater pops the skateboard into the air with his or her feet

stalefish grab
an aerial move where the skater reaches his or her back arm behind his or her leg and grabs the middle of the board

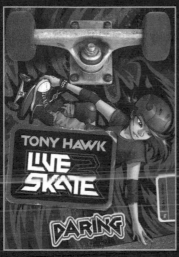

HOW DO YOU LIVE?

written by
BRANDON TERRELL

Brandon Terrell is the author of numerous children's books, including six volumes in the Tony Hawk's 900 Revolution series and several Sports Illustrated Kids graphic novels. When not hunched over his laptop writing, Brandon enjoys watching movies, reading, baseball, and spending time with his wife and two children.

pencils and colors by
FERNANDO CANO

Fernando Cano is an all-around artist living in Monterrey, Mexico. He currently works as a concept artist for the video game company CGbot. Having published with Marvel, DC, Pathfinder, and IDW, he spends his free time playing video games, singing, writing, and above all, drawing!

inks by
SERGIO MARTINEZ

Illustrator Sergio Martinez has a background in animated character and background development and comic illustration for Marvel, IDW, and Stone Arch Books. He currently works as a video game concept artist for CGbot in Monterrey, Mexico. He also spends his free time playing video games, watching movies, and arguing with his friends.